Me

D0520538

JUST ME AND MY DAD

BY
MERCER MAYER

🎚 A GOLDEN BOOK • NEW YORK

ISBN 0-307-11839-8   www.goldenbooks.com
Printed in the United States of America   First Random House Edition 2003

We went camping,
just me and my dad.
Dad drove the car
because I'm too little.

I picked the campsite, but someone
was already living there.
So I gave it back.

We found another
campsite nearby.
My dad was tired,
so I pitched the tent.

We made a campfire.
I found the wood,
and my dad lit the fire.

I wanted to take my dad
for a ride in our canoe,
but I launched it too hard.

We went fishing instead.

My dad took a snapshot
of the fish we caught.
Then I cooked dinner
for me and my dad.

We had eggs.

After dinner, I told my dad a ghost story.
Boy, did he get scared!

I gave my dad a big hug.
That made him feel better.

Then we went to bed.

I stayed up with my dad and let him read a story to me.

We slept in our tent all night long—
just me and my dad.